D1152188

IMAGINE THAT

Licensed exclusively to Imagine That Publishing Ltd
Tide Mill Way, Woodbridge, Suffolk, IP12 1AP, UK
www.imaginethat.com
Copyright © 2021 Imagine That Group Ltd
All rights reserved
4 6 8 9 7 5 3
Manufactured in China

Written by Susie Linn
Illustrated by Alex Patrick

All rights reserved. No part of this publication may be reproduced, stored in a retrieval system, or transmitted in any form or by any means, electronic, mechanical, photocopying, recording or otherwise, without the prior written permission of the publisher. Neither this book nor any part or any of the illustrations, photographs or reproductions contained in it shall be sold or disposed of otherwise than as a complete book, and any unauthorised sale of such part illustration, photograph or reproduction shall be deemed to be a breach of the publisher's copyright.

ISBN 978-1-80105-004-3

A catalogue record for this book is available from the British Library

Be
HAPPY!

Written by Susie Linn
Illustrated by Alex Patrick

One day, Little Bear looked
up at Mummy Bear and said,
'When I grow up, what will I be?'

'You can be anything!'
said Mummy Bear.

'Come with me and
I'll show you.

You can be kind ...
and helpful and true.

GRANDAD'S DEN

You can be strong ...
in all that you do.

You can
be fast ...

and race to the top.

You can be slow ...

and know when
to stop.

You can be playful ...

and have lots of fun.

You can be calm ...
when each day is done.

You can be brave ...

and try out new things.

You can be honest ...
whatever life brings.

You can be
curious ...

and always
explore.

You can be loving ...
give hugs evermore.

Even better than this,
any time, anywhere ...

... you can be happy,
my dear Little Bear.'